The A·B·Cs of D&D

Written by Ivan Van Norman
Illustrated by Caleb Cleveland

A is for ADVENTURE.

Our journey has begun!

B is for BOOK,

the source of all our fun!

C is for CREATURES

of every shape and size.

E is for ENCHANTMENT,
magic that helps us do our best!

F is for FRIENDSHIP,
the best reward
for quests.

I is for IMAGINATION.

What's YOUR favorite tale?

J is for JOURNEY.

Time to wander down the trail.

K is for KINGDOM.

Let's explore, discover, and roam.

L is for LOST, so it's time
to head for home.

M is for MYSTERY, which can begin with a stone.

N is for NATURE and its wonders still unknown.

O is for OWLBEAR,

which you won't find in a zoo!

P is for PLANNING,

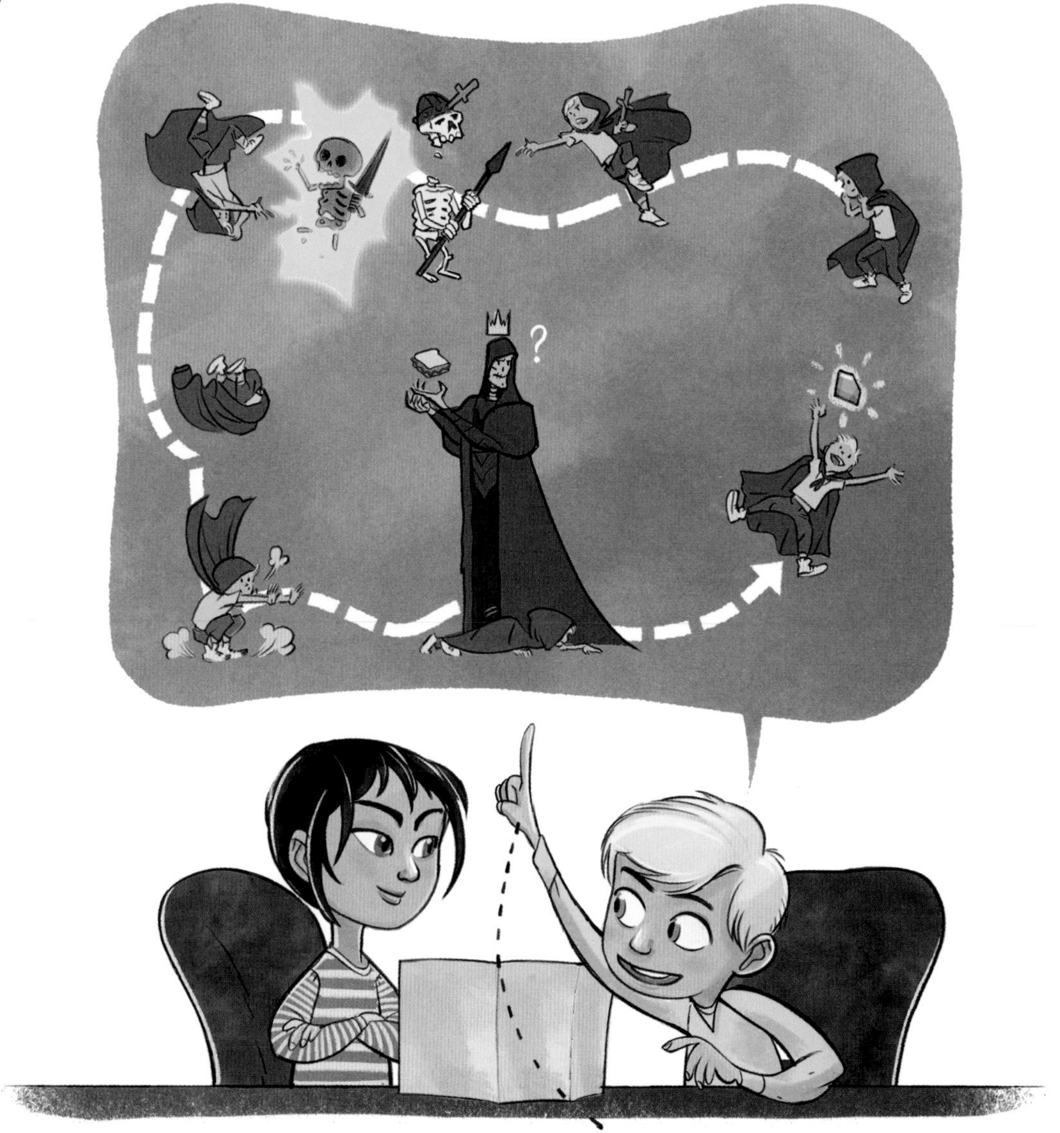

so what do you want to do?

Q is for QUEST,

an adventure we can share.

R is for RAVENLOFT,
where spooky stories scare.

S is for SHIP.

Let's all go for a ride!

T is for TREASURE,

the sweet stuff monsters hide.

U is for UNDERDARK,

where legends
lie untold.

V is for VILLAINS,

either cowardly or bold.

W is for WISDOM,

a trait most essential.

Z is for ZEAL,